# The Rabbit Who Couldn't Find His Daddy

Lilian Edvall
Pictures by Sara Gimbergsson

Translated by
Elisabeth Kallick Dyssegaard

R&S
BOOKS

Stockholm  New York  London  Adelaide  Tor

Rabbit woke with a start.
Mommy was there and Little Sister was there,
but someone was missing.
Rabbit began searching right away, because
all of a sudden he missed his daddy a lot.

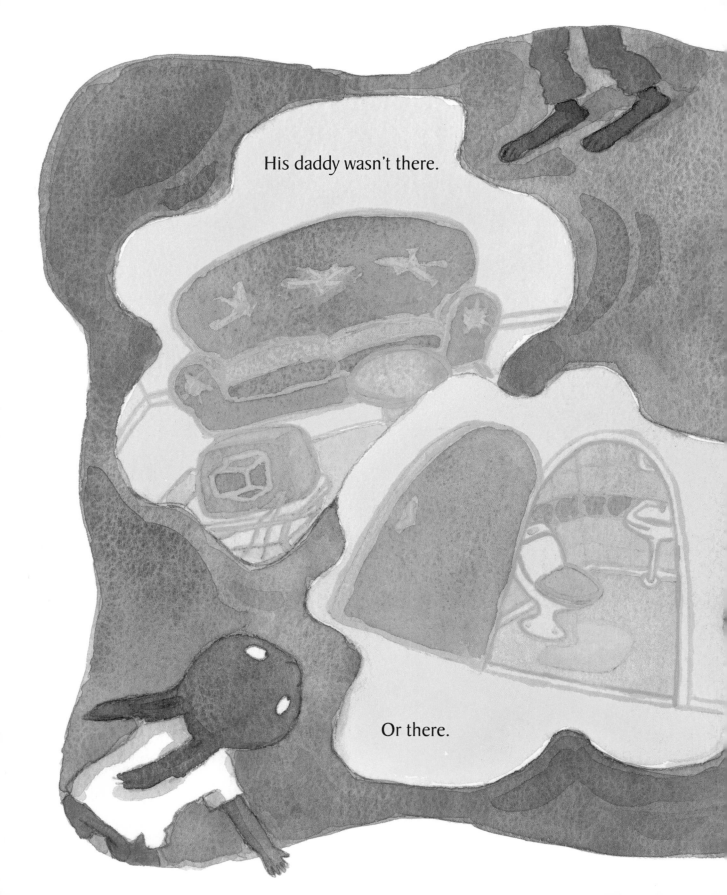

His daddy wasn't there.

Or there.

Or there.

"Mommy," whispered Rabbit, "Daddy's missing."

Mommy sat up sleepily. She looked at the clock, she looked at Rabbit, then she yawned.

"Daddy probably went to sleep in your bed," she said.

Of course, thought Rabbit. He had forgotten to look there.

"Come snuggle up," said Mommy, making room for him under the covers. But Rabbit just wanted to be with his daddy, and he shook his head so hard that his ears tickled his nose. Mommy sighed and went back to sleep.

Now Little Sister woke up, bright-eyed and bushy-tailed.

"Daddy is missing," said Rabbit seriously.

"How exciting," said Little Sister, who loved adventures.

Rabbit was annoyed. It wasn't exciting at all.

"But I think I know where he is," he said.

"Come on, let's go look," said Little Sister.

"Okeydokey," said Rabbit. That's what his teacher said at preschool.

"I think he's in my room," whispered Rabbit.
"Okeydokey," said Little Sister, and they carefully
opened the door. They found lots of stuff but no Daddy.
"Yippee," said Little Sister, and she jumped up and
down. "Daddy is playing hide-and-seek."
"No, he's not," said Rabbit.

"But look," said Little Sister, and picked up the belt to Daddy's robe. "He <u>has</u> been here. We'll look some more."
"Or we'll ask Mommy again," said Rabbit.
"Nah, she's sleeping," said Little Sister.

"We have to think," said Rabbit.
"Why did Daddy leave a clue?
And what's he doing now?"

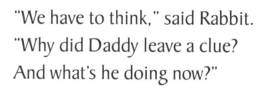

Little Sister thought hard.

"Maybe he went out to buy carrots," she said finally.

"Unlikely," said Rabbit. "But we could check if the car is still there."

"No," said Little Sister. "It's parked next to the garage. I'm scared to go out there when it's dark."

"But maybe I'm not," said Rabbit.

Little Sister looked admiringly at her big brother.

Rabbit opened the front door but closed it again right away.
Outside, one lonely streetlamp was lit; the wind shook the trees.
"Are you scared?" asked Little Sister.
"No, of course not. Something just blew in my eye," said Rabbit.
Then he gathered his courage and opened the door again.

This time he'd made up his mind:
he was going to race out to the garage.
"Promise to stay right here," he said to
Little Sister, and took off.

Just then, the front door slammed. And locked.
Little Sister began to cry.
"Help," she said. "I think I saw a ghost."
"There are no ghosts," said Rabbit.
"What about a haunting hare?" asked Little Sister.
"There are almost no haunting hares either," said
Rabbit, looking around nervously.

"We'll call Mommy," said Rabbit.
And they did.
And since no one could scream louder than Little Sister,
it sounded pretty impressive.
The lights went on in the house, in one room after another.

"Mommy," they screamed again, and now the outside light was also
turned on. Mommy opened the door; her fur was all rumpled.
"Sweeties," she said, "what <u>are</u> you doing here?"
"We're looking for Daddy," said Rabbit.
"Looking for Daddy?" Mommy repeated, confused.
"I'm freezing," Little Sister said, shivering.
"Well, come back inside," said Mommy, "and warm up."

Just then, the door to the basement stairs opened.
Out stepped Daddy. Rabbit threw himself into his arms.
"Daddy, Daddy, where've you been?" he asked.
"Um . . . You're all up in the middle of the night?" asked Daddy.
"Yep," said Little Sister. "We're playing hide-and-seek."

"You didn't answer me," said Rabbit. "Where have you been?"

"Well," said Daddy, still looking surprised to see the whole family. "This is how it was. I couldn't sleep. And it was so crowded in my bed that I went to sleep in yours."

"I know," said Rabbit.

"Really?" asked Daddy, looking puzzled.

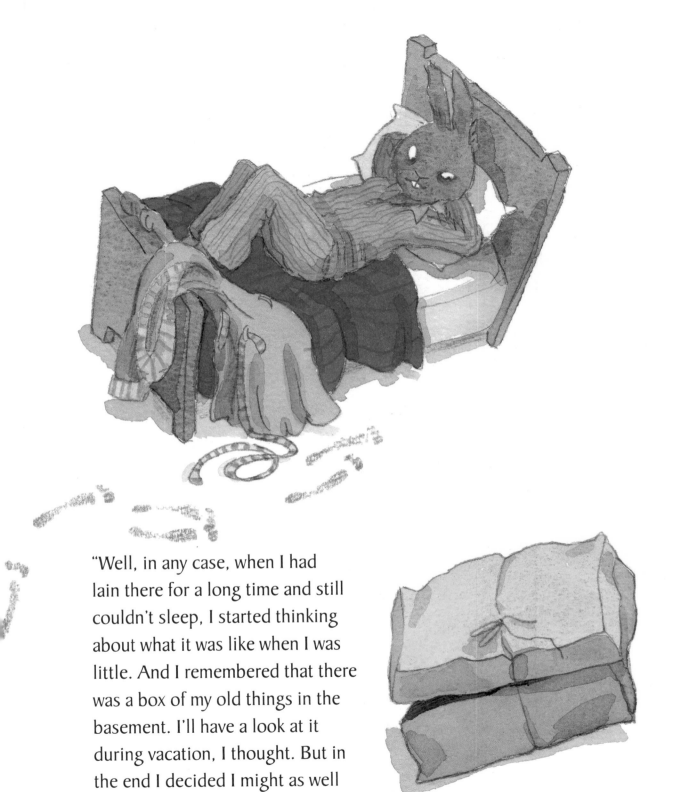

"Well, in any case, when I had
lain there for a long time and still
couldn't sleep, I started thinking
about what it was like when I was
little. And I remembered that there
was a box of my old things in the
basement. I'll have a look at it
during vacation, I thought. But in
the end I decided I might as well
do it right then."

"I sneaked down as quietly as I could. I didn't want to wake you up."

"Did you find anything?" Rabbit wondered.

"Yes, indeed," said Daddy secretively.

"What?" asked Rabbit.

"We'll look tomorrow," said Mommy.

"No, let's do it now," said Rabbit.

"Yes, yes, yes, now," said Little Sister.

And then they all followed Daddy down to the basement.
A half-open box sat on the top shelf.
Daddy reached up and pulled something out of it. A worn,
grayish stuffed animal, a little lamb.

"Look," said Daddy proudly. "This was my favorite stuffed animal when I was little. I always had to have it in my bed. It had to lie on my pillow and it had to look at me . . ."

"That one?" asked Rabbit. "But it's so dirty."

"And it's missing an ear," said Little Sister.

"It's not exactly new-looking," said Mommy.

Daddy looked at them with surprise. And at the lamb.

"But it's so nice," he said, looking hurt.

"Well, in any case, it's time to go to bed."

He put the lamb back in the box with a sigh.
"I thought it was kind of nice," said Rabbit.
"We could keep it . . . on the hat shelf."
"Hmmm," said Daddy. But he seemed happier.
And he picked up the lamb again.

"What should we do now?" asked Mommy.
"Go to bed or drink hot chocolate?"
Mommy turned on a light, and Daddy
brought out the mugs even though it was
the middle of the night.
"Aren't you tired?" asked Daddy.
"No," said Rabbit.
"No," said Little Sister.
There was a thud when she fell asleep with
her head against the lamb.
Mommy carried her off to bed.

But Daddy and Rabbit stayed up for a while talking.
"I think there might be one more box," said Daddy.